Fragile Wrappings

A collection of 12 short stories
for adults

Dianne Bates

Contents

Fragile Wrappings

It is Tuesday, two days before Payday in suburban Anywhere, the day Norma and her friends flock to their promise of Paradise.

"Mike's the caller today," says Norma. "He's my favourite."

"Mine too," say neighbours Doreen and Maisie.

Responding to absences in their lives they assemble with the others, nameless housewives, figures swollen with carbohydrates and children. Pregnant with gossip, they wait for Mike's call in the Westfield landscape, beneath signs promising Fantasy Donuts, Jean Connection and Mr Whippy, between musak and echoes of "Today's specials", among smells of cash and coffee, ice-cream, fresh bread, fairy floss, the air ripe with expectation.Now Mike addresses them, calls them to attention. "Green card, number 30, eyes down, first game." They respond. And he is away, thrusting numbers at them:

legs eleven

88, two fat ladies, wobble-wobble

halfway there, 45

two little ducks, 22

unlucky for some, 13

- diving deeper for numbers until that moment when one in the number-randy mass of women, shrieks, in orgasmic eureka:

"BINGO!"

And a collective sigh is released from the mouths of losers and they voice their frustrations:

"Gee, that was quick,"

"I was so close."

"If only he'd called six, that's all I wanted."

Norma reaches for her cigarettes, a ritual when the business is done.

"Numbers' right," Mike declares. And the Chosen One accepts the cash. Twenty dollars. With careful indifference, she slips it down the front of her dress, reaches for her cards. Next game. Perhaps she can score again. You never know. Some do.

"The bitch, she won last week ... some people have all the luck." The losers mutter among themselves. Some suspect a conspiracy. But they do not leave. Instead, it's all eyes down as Mike begins again:

on its own, number 7

any way you look at it, 69

retiring age, 65...

"BINGO!"

Another satisfied customer. And the others, clicking tongues, ripping cards, complaining.

"Three!" exclaims Maisie. "I only had three left ... 26, 42, 63. I waited so long for those three it's ridiculous."

The morning seems to give a sigh, stirs itself, loosens tongues.

"Dulcie's a grannie now, didn't you know?" says Doreen. "A lovely little girl. Kylie. She looks after her while her daughter's at work. That's why you don't see her at Bingo any more."

Norma and her friends share toffees, peeling back the fragile wrappings of their lives while the numbers are checked. "Bruce's going away to Queanbeyan next week, then to Canberra. I says to him, 'D'you know where Dapto is, Bruce?'"

"Got your raffle tickets, ladies?" Mike intones. "You've got to be in it to win it."

Now they cast eyes upwards to their god. Let it be me, Norma prays. We could do with the meat tray, what with the barbecue on for our Jamie's 21st next month.

All around her the unspoken thoughts:

The night out at the restaurant, now that'd be good ...so long since the old man took me anywhere.

Any prize, just something to show for the day...

Let it be me, let it be me.

"This week," Mike declares, "the Crepes Place has donated lunches to the value of twelve dollars. And we've a breadbasket here donated from Fielders Fresh Breasts..."

Breasts! Did you hear that? He said "Breasts."

Mike blushes, his face ripening as the sea of breasts before him - the shapeless, the pendulous, the child-wearied, the stretch-marked - rises and quivers. Mirth fills gaps in the musak, unites the girls, gives focus to their drifting day. Prize winner or not, each has plucked this moment to share with her family when next they are united under a common roof. They want it to last forever.

It doesn't, of course, the raffles are drawn.

"I never win," Norma mumbles to herself, as the game resumes. Lick the pencil, eyes down, cross the numbers, feel the tension climaxing as the squares are reduced to three, then two, then one. And she waits, waits with dry mouth and mounting heart beat as the numbers are called:

thirty six

twenty four

legs eleven

all on its own, number 3...

"BINGO!"

And then to curse a loser's fate. Only one left, to be so close, to miss out by only one. Why not me, each asks herself. But there is no time now to dwell on lost opportunities. Next game, eyes down, last game.

Another winner and all possibilities for this week exhausted. The morning has withdrawn. Now they straggle out, Norma and the others, to return to afternoon soap operas, to pot-filled sinks and brimming laundry baskets, to the opening of after-school doors, to all that shapes their ordinary lives. Yet some will be able to look into mirrors and see the face of a winner, will have had this day set apart from all the other dull days of their lives. And later, called by the hour to their bed, they will boast to their dour, grey men, "I won at Bingo today." Then, snoring lightly, they will dream of their day, the best time for ages.

Getting There

1. The Shortest Journey

We are in a black sedan travelling to the crematorium. I sit in the rear seat with David and our daughter, Claire. In the front is the driver and beside him, in the passenger's seat, is the coffin, small and shiny and unadorned.

Inside the coffin is the body of my youngest child, Kathleen.

The journey, like Kathleen's life, is short. We drive through the ordinary outer suburb on an unremarkable road. Tears blur my vision. All I can see is my baby's tiny body. And her head, swollen and unrecognisable after the operation. That day, that dread-filled day. After. I stroked her hair, kissed her soft, still-warm cheeks and held her hand which would never carry a spouse's ring, or push her nipple to a baby's mouth, or become mottled and old.

The crematorium, white as a wedding cake. Mourners, too few for such a large life.

Unsteady and reluctant, my feet touch the ground. I take Claire's hand and move forward to words of condolence. I do not hear. Walk into the last place where I will ever see my baby. Down the aisle to a seat, hard and wooden as my heart. Watch as the coffin is placed on view. Become aware of the preacher droning platitudes, offering prayers to the god that allowed my child to die. See her coffin disappearing behind a blood-red curtain.

It is over. The funeral car takes us back to the house which was once a home.

2. New Beginnings

In the first year of our relationship, Max and I decide to live on the South Coast. We buy a trailer and fill it and our car with essentials. This includes Claire who is to sleep for most of the 500 km trip. It is night when we depart, city lights soon switching off as we speed away, the darkness of country swallowing us.

"Sleepy?" Max asks solicitously.

I am, in fact, wide awake. This is a journey that will start a whole new life. As a child I'd lived in the country, had sworn to never again live there. In a crisis there are no neighbours, no doctors, no hospitals. Country quietness screams at me: I crave cities.

Inside the car is warm and cosy. I feel like an astronaut rocketing through space with whole galaxies to explore.

Max and I glance at one another and smile. He's lived before on The Diggings, Dr George Mountain, Tanja via Bega. Alone, he says. And he's always wanted a woman to share his life with him there. He talks about the forest, the wild creatures, a boat he is building that sits atop the mountain perched as though ready to launch into a gulley.

I forget about my abhorrence of country. Think only of a new life. Eventually I slump in my seat, and, exhausted from a long day of packing, fall asleep. When I awake, the road is bumpy. Trees stretch forward as if to devour us.

I peer ahead at the winding track, ask myself how steep is the mountain that we are now climbing. Hope that we will not spear off into the wilderness below before we have reached where we are going. Rain slashes the windscreen; the wipers work frantically.

Before long the headlights reveal a house by the side of the road.

"We're here," Max announces.

I sit in the car as he lumbers through knee-high grass, his torchlight slicing into the darkness and then alighting on a faded blue door. Watch as he vanishes inside. Follow his light winking through a side window. Watch as he returns to me, water shiny on his face.

"It's a mess," he says. "But we'll make it into a home pretty soon."

We drag our bedding into the tiny hut. Use newspapers to sweep away rat droppings. Then, exhausted, we collapse onto the cleared floor as rain belts onto the tin roof.

Max and my daughter sleep. I lay awake; wonder what I have let myself in for.

3. The Best time

So my only daughter marries in Hawaii and I find out about it six months later. She's come back to Australia from an overseas' trip where she's met Benoit, dumped her de facto partner of three years and made plans to live in Canada. All without telling me.

From her fifteenth year our relationship has been rocky; she's despised me for years. Now, however, she invites me to visit her. And to meet her husband.

Before long I am on a plane to Vancouver via Japan, thence on to Ottawa where Claire and Benoit have made their home.

Overnight at Narida airport hotel, unable to sleep, I watch TV. A group of middle-aged Japanese women is travelling around their country going from bathhouse to restaurant to bathhouse. The countryside is exquisite. The idea of a holiday featuring eating, soaking in mineral springs, and sleeping is tempting. I wish my journey could finish this night; that I could find a similar tour and join it.

Arriving in Ottawa, I meet the stoic-faced husband; try to make conversation with him. Try to rekindle with Claire the happy days of her childhood. Fail on both counts. Take the newly-weds out to dinner, buy them bedding; pay far too much. No thanks, but then I haven't really expected any.

Claire and I journey together to Old Quebec. We talk, we laugh, mend broken fences.

Back in Ottawa, I learn she is to depart that week for a month-long holiday to Ireland, a spur-of-the-moment decision.

Not wanting to stay alone with my reticent son-in-law, I leave for New York City. There, alone and unencumbered, I have the best time.

Bumming a Lift

The prison farm where my loved one is incarcerated is three hours by car from where I live. Once a month I walk to the bottom of the mountain pass, stick out my thumb and wait for a stranger's kindness.

This weekend rain is predicted, and the air is chilled, the sky growling. The first leg is easy. The driver says – as they all do: "Hitching's not safe, you know, young lady. There are all kinds of weirdos on the roads these days."

"I never have problems," I reply. And it's true. Sometimes a driver will even go out of his way, for instance, taking me from the highway down the dirt track to the farm, about three kilometres.

Dropped off at the first crossroad, I wave my gratitude. And turn to wait for the next vehicle. A car-full of youths stops but I don't accept their lift. I'm suspicious of men my own age, especially those that travel, like wolves, in packs. It's the solitary driver I prefer. That way I'm not out numbered.

The next driver looks innocuous. He smiles, asks my destination, gestures for me to hop in. As I've done so often before, dozens of times, I accept the invitation.

For the first few kilometres we make small talk, but I notice his eyes keep shifting from the road sideways to my bare knee.

"Got a boy-friend?" he asks.

"Sure."

"So why isn't he driving you places?"

"He's working this weekend."

The driver works the gear stick, revs the engine. His hand reaches towards mine, poises above it. I move away, thinking it's time to put my escape plan into motion.

"He's a police officer," I lie.

His hand returns to the steering wheel.

We drive on further, moving away from a town into open country. Further along there's an untarred side road. He steers towards it.

"This isn't the way." My voice is steady.

"It's a short cut," he explains.

"If you don't get back onto the main road, I'm jumping out," I say, determined. I open the door.

The car slows and then, engine still running, brakes to a stop.

"Get out," he commands.

Gladly I do as he says, stand back and watch as he chucks a uey, accelerating at great speed away from me, dust rising behind him in sheets of anger.

I breathe a sigh of relief and, when my heart has calmed, walk back to the bypass. There I once again put out my thumb and wait for another ride.

Years later I'm with my husband driving along the highway late one Saturday night in our local town. There are people everywhere, mostly young, shouting, laughing, some staggering.

A group of girls, not one of them older than my 15 year old who is home in bed, steps onto the road. Several hold up stop-sign hands. Can't stand the thought of teenage girls stranded late at night out with all kinds of lurking danger. We oblige.

"Want a lift? I ask.

"Thanks," says one. She slides into the backseat. Three friends follow. The air is instantly thick with cheap perfume.

"Going far?

One of them names a town about five kay away. It is their last communication with us. They chat about the disco they've just been to. Giggle drunkenly among themselves. Forget that Bill and I are in the front seat.

At the designated town, one says, "Here will do" as if to a taxi driver.

They clamber out without as much as a backwards' glance.

A week later.

He stands at the side of the road in the middle of nowhere, gesturing. The trip has been uneventful; a stranger will be welcome relief from my own company.

I stop, reach over and open the passenger's front door. "Going far?" I ask.

He doesn't reply. Instead, steps into the car and sits down.

Picking him up is a mistake. I know it immediately.

He stinks. Of shit.

He turns away from me, to look towards where he had been standing. I glance at him, his hair grey and matted; his coat grimy and torn. Notice his hands, age-mottled and gnarled, scratching at one another in his lap.

"Where are you off to?" I ask loudly, determined to have him speak.

He doesn't answer. Instead, he looks towards the road ahead. His hands tumble in his lap, snatching at one another. He rocks his body, back and forth, like a metronome on speed.

Should I accelerate away, or turf him out as quickly as I've invited him in?

Good manners prevail. I rev the engine and shoot back onto the highway. Fifty kays to the nearest town.

Once again I try to engage him. "Been waiting long?"

Nothing. Just the smell of shit seeping into my pores, turning my stomach.

I imagine. He is a rapist. A killer. A serial killer.

My car eats the road. A cannibal serial killer.

"Mind if I play some music?" I ask. As if it is his right to make choices in my car, in my space.

When he remains silent, I flick the switch, try to relax to the joyous beat of a South American pipe band. The music seems to agitate him even more.

Fleetingly, he turns to look at me. His face is unreadable.

Every second I wrestle with my conscience. It isn't right to abandon him: I have made a contract to take him. Somewhere.

Conscience wins. Despite my panic, my fear, my wild imagination, I continue driving. Don't even ask him to fasten his safety belt.

When I stop on the outskirts of town and say, "Here's a good place to catch another ride," he climbs out without a backward glance.

I drive on, promising myself to never again trust strangers on roads.

Graffiti on a Toilet Wall

Alone. Again. When was I ever so alone? The hostel, normally filled with the bustle of residents, is now empty. Silence squeezes into every nook, hangs heavily, like the sleeping hour of midnight. Everyone, except for me, has left for the weekend to see family or friends. Even Miss Dobie, the caretaker, is in her room, most likely having a nap.

I wander aimlessly, along the hall past bedrooms, down the stairs (sliding on the bannister), across the lobby and into the dining room with its post-meal beefy smell, and then into the common room. There I sink into an armchair and absorb the Saturday afternoon ambience. Most evenings this room buzzes with conversations, the girls gossiping, usually about boys, the television burbling in the background. Sometimes, bored with my own company, I come here hoping to engage someone. Sure, girls nod or smile at me, but it's rare that anyone takes the time for a chat. Recently I saw a photograph that I really identified with — it was a single tree on an endless plain, bending towards the ground. That's how I feel most of the time these days – alone. Like that tree. Alone, like I am this afternoon.

Even at work I feel alienated. The other office girls have their cliques, none of which include me. And, since I decided to leave home for good, divorcing myself from my unbearable family – my belligerent father, mouse-like mother and argumentative brother – I have found myself more alone that I've ever been in my life.

Last week when I was in a public toilet stall, I saw someone had scratched, 'I hate myself' on the back of the door. These three sad words cheered me in a way. I might be alone and friendless, but I honestly can't say I hate myself. Poor girl. How awful it must be to hate yourself. I would like to meet that anonymous scribbler and find out what she hates in herself. The way I see it, is that if you can't like yourself, how can you expect others to like you? Perhaps if I could talk to that girl, we could become friends.

The silence in the hostel has become oppressive, and, not wanting to become overwhelmed by it, I take the sudden decision to go down the street.

Outside, the sky is grey with wall-to-wall clouds, the street empty of people. Wanting to speak with someone, I decide I'll surely find company in the nearby milk bar.

I'm not in luck. There are no customers except for the server. Slumped on a stool behind the counter, he is scruffy, and young like myself, about eighteen. He's busy texting on his phone and doesn't look up until I move to stand directly in front of him. When he lifts his head, I flash my most beguiling smile.

I had hoped for even a glimmer of friendliness, but his face is immobile until he grunts, 'Yeah?'

'A Diet Coke, please,' I say, again with a smile.

He gestures behind me to a fridge.

I help myself and offer him a five dollar note. 'It's pretty quiet today,' I say, twisting the lid. 'I don't suppose you've had many customers.'

I hadn't expected him to wax lyrical and tell me the story of his life, but it seems he doesn't hear me as his attention is once again on his phone.

'Well, yeah, nice talking to you,' I say sarcastically as I exit the shop.

As I meander down the street sipping my coke, my mind returns to the anonymous graffitist. Why would she hate herself, I wonder? Is it because others have demeaned her, and she's accepted their bullying? I find it so sad that someone can write their deepest feeling for everyone to see, but not to speak it to a single other person. *I* don't hate myself: I have some virtues – kindness, generosity, compassion – but sometimes, especially times like today – I wonder if it's as though I am carrying a sign that reads 'Ignore me'. Or perhaps I have 'Invisible Girl' tattooed on my forehead.

Now I am not only alone, but a creature feels as though it's creeping into my being, lodging itself in my heart, and my gut, a creature with the name of Loneliness. How I yearn not just for company, but for someone to see me, really see me. And, would it be too much to ask, for someone to actually touch me, put their hand in mind – and, dare I even think it – pull me towards them and hug me?

It has started to rain. At first there's a drizzle, but within minutes it has given way to heavy drops, the rain sheeting, across in front of me. Unless I seek cover, I'll be drenched. It's not so far back to the hostel, so, squealing and pulling my coat over my head, I race towards it, splashing through puddles as the rain falls heavier.

Outside the hostel stands a sodden teenager, her arms wrapped around herself for warmth. She smiles at my approach. 'Do you live here?' she asks.

I nod as I put the key in the door. 'Come in, you look soaked,' I say.

She grabs her suitcase and wheels it into the lobby, puddles following her across the tiled floor. 'I kept ringing,' she says, 'but no-one came to the door.'

'Well, you're safe now,' I say with a smile. 'If you'd like to wait a moment, I'll get you a towel so you can dry yourself off.'

I rush back from my room and she's drying her dripping hair when Miss Dobie appears. 'I thought I heard someone at the door.' To the girl: 'You must be Josie?'

The girl nods as the office phone rings.

'I need to answer that,' Miss Dobie says. 'Mikki, would you take Josie to Room 14?'

Of course, I'm only too willing to have something to occupy my time.

Josie chats to me as we climb the stairs to the bedrooms. She tells me where she's come from – the central coast — and why she's moving into the hostel – to attend the local university. This is the longest anyone has spoken to me in days, maybe even weeks.

In room 14 I sit on Josie's bed and watch as she unpacks her bag. She isn't at all tidy, jamming clothes into drawers and tossing books and pens onto the desk. I notice a red plastic folder covered with scribbles, drawings, declarations of love. And slogans such as *Be kind to yourself. Today is the start of your life. Girls rule!* All the slogans are positive; this is not a girl who hates herself; rather, she seems high-spirited and feisty. I draw that conclusion, too, from her steady stream of spoken words as she skates through what seems like a happy, busy life, full of loving family and many friends. Nobody has talked to me this much for months, perhaps for a year or more.

'Of course,' she says, I don't know a single soul in Wollongong. Except you, of course.' She pauses and gave me a quizzical look. Don't you have something to do, some place to go?

'Sure,' I say, rising.

'I need to have a shower…'

'I'm outa here.'

Josie shuts the door almost as soon as I'm through it.

I'm halfway down the hall when her door opens again. 'Hey,' Josie calls.

I turn.

'What's your name again?'

The Farmer's Wife

She's a farmer's wife and he's a Vietnam vet. His war-time experiences define – and rule – their lives, create a way of being that the politicians who sent him to war would never suspect. Or know. They would never, for instance, have predicted that this country-born and bred girl married the farmer shortly before he was conscripted, to become a war victim decades after the troops were withdrawn.

She's a typical country woman with straw-textured hair, peppery grey because now she is middle-aged and never bothers with – never had time for – hair-dye. Or make-up, for that, which most likely accounts for her skin – coarse and sun-spotted, her nose red-veined; her eyes, red too from over-exposure to the sun.

Today she rises at 6 am, as she always does, and dresses in jeans, cotton shirt and sensible leather boots. She does not own a dressing gown for that would imply laziness and she is never lazy. In the kitchen she makes tea, strong-leaved and served piping hot with fresh cream and two sugars, just how he likes it. It is now that he comes indoors with a pail of steaming milk from the house cow. As always, she greets him cheerfully, but today he does not reply. Nor does he acknowledge her presence. She is used to his moods, to his frequent silences.

Soon she plans to depart the farm, to drive three hours to the nearest town to meet city friends who are passing through. A week ago, in a better mood, he had agreed to go with her. But today she knows he does not want company. Even hers. She is used to him withdrawing into a mental space that allows no room for others. On days like today his head is swamped with war and at night in sleep he replays battles.

Last night was thin-mooned. But madness does not need a full moon, and he cried wildly, bucking until the bed was a tank ramming enemy. "Kill the bastards! Kill them!" he had cried again and again, his sweat, like blood, drenching bed-clothes. He woke, as he often does, in a lather of terror. Then, as always, he cannot face further death-impaled sleep and so he rises. Sits on the veranda starring across the drought-scarred paddocks. And broods.

Lately, rain has blessed the land, bringing with it hope. "I think I'll plough the back paddock," he had said the day before. "Just in case." Meaning, just in case more rain falls and germinates new pasture. So ploughing is today's plan, his promise forgotten. She dares not ask him if he wishes to change his mind for all questions at times like this are grenades, all suggestions minefields.

She watches as he plants his Akubra on his balding head where red hair once sprouted, thick and lush, sets down the milk for her to strain, and exits the kitchen. The screen-wire door thuds behind him against the frame as it has dozens of times a day, day in, day out, for the thirty and more years of their married life.

The milk now treated and refrigerated, she turns her hand to making biscuits. A gift for her friends. She does not see them often, just now and again when she visits interstate to see her sister. He never goes with her, preferring the familiarity, the routine, the absence of stress that is here on the land of his forebears. As she mixes the dough, she hears the tractor revving, glances past the home garden, past the hen-yard and the wood-pile. He is slouched on the seat, eyes ahead to the sky, measuring the clouds. All days here are measured by the sky, by its blueness, its bruise of cloud or lack thereof. Days pass, each rolling on from the last into the next and nothing much changes except the seasons and the weather they bring. The heat. Or winds. Or coldness. And this – the real blessing – the elixir of rain.

When her biscuits are baked and cooled, she packs them in plastic and puts them into a pretty bag bought especially for the occasion. Then she locates two pair of binoculars – one borrowed from her son on the adjoining property – and goes to the four-wheel drive in the garage. She does not - in fact, never does - lock the house, though she checks before leaving to see there is beer in the fridge. He likes a chilled can after a long day driving around the paddocks. Sometimes, she returns from trips to town or further afield to find him disoriented and morose from too much drink. It is then that she leads him to bed where the warmth of their touching releases the hard knot of his anger. It is then, in the bosom of his vulnerability, that she renews her vow to be faithful, to never leave him, though God knows she often enough thinks of it, especially on those days when something – anything – triggers his rage. When he becomes incomprehensible and lashes out. He has never struck her, but many a time he has prowled the house and the property armed with a gun. She has seen him shoot a dog for barking, another for not obeying a command. On such days she sees the madness in his soul and fears for her life. And yet he can be so charming. The Bowling Club ladies love him; shower him with tokens of affection – home-cooked goodies and hand-made sweaters. They tell her how lucky she is to have him. And perhaps she is, though sometimes he is an anchor that threatens to drown her.

As she drives down the home track, sheets of dust enveloping the car, she waves to him, but if he sees her, he does not acknowledge her departure. Behind him the ground churns. Furrows grow long and straight.

She drives for hours on a road she knows as intimately as the back of her strong, speckled hands. Past land red brown for nearly a year but now weed-green and pregnant with seasonal promise. Past grass parrots and cockatoos celebrating rain, and filled dams, and cattle which have escaped low-sale prices, and which will now line farmers' pockets at market. As she drives, the woman reflects on her life.

Up until a year ago she had been a principal, but petty school politics and stress had forced her early retirement. At the time her head was filled with plans – to study, to start a home business, to write. But her husband's needs – and the drought –forced her to change direction. Unable to face debt and drenched with hopelessness many farmers faced days that vacuumed their spirits. A woman on the land needed to be more indomitable than ever, needed to be the rock on which her man could cling until the rains come.

Then, when the land was drenched and dirt turned to mud, there were animals to be saved. Single-handed she had used the tractor and thick rope to pull poddy heifers from mud-holes. And here, on the road, she and a woman passenger had only last week released a young bull from the entanglement of a wire fence it had failed to jump. Yes, she is a farmer's wife. That is her role. Nothing else beckons now. Or in the future.

The town is ahead and now a sense of trepidation creeps into the woman. It is a long time since she has seen her friends. She wonders if they will have enough conversation to pass the hours planned for their meeting. Away from the companionship of school colleagues, sequestered for months on the farm, much of the time alone or in the company of his silences, she feels dry of wit and words. But there, her friends are waiting near the town hall, their vehicle parked at an odd angle at the kerb. She waves and they respond likewise, seeming to be enthusiastic at seeing her. Her spirit lifts. She brakes and climbs down from the cabin.

"How wonderful to see you!" Her friend rushes across the road and embraces her. She feels the warmth of her body, her lips brushing her cheek, and something in her melts, relaxes.

"Did you have a good trip?" her friend's husband asks. She likes him. He is strong and caring. Quiet, too, but it is a natural shyness, something that attracts her to him. His wife is more outgoing, talks far too much. But it doesn't matter.

She offers the biscuits which are exclaimed over. "I couldn't cook to save my soul," says the woman. "Thanks so much. Very thoughtful of you."

The man offers her a gift of red wine – his favourite – and a book he has written which has won awards. He's autographed it, too, and she's touched by his kind words.

Down the main street they amble, looking for a cafe that is open this Sunday afternoon. The city woman chats on about the trip. "I hate the country," she says, "as well you know."

Yes, her friend has made it clear that country life is never for her. She's been raised on the land and clearly prefers city living. "There are no decent doctors in the country. Or cinemas. Or theatre. Or..."

On and on she goes with her list.

I wish I could articulate the reasons why I stay, the farmer's wife thinks. She knows then, knows how the land has grown around her bones, is part of her, as essential as breathing. But she says nothing. Just listens. She is a good listener.

When the afternoon tea is finished in the only open cafe, the three of them pile into her four-wheel drive and she takes them on a tour. There's an industrial area, hectares of orchards, the sports ground, the usual country town attractions. Then she drives them to the top of the mountain overlooking the town and surrounding countryside. There her friends look at the panorama through binoculars and she points out significant landmarks.

Her woman friend stands on a small stone wall and is startled when a wallaby bounds towards her.

"My God!" the woman says, "I thought he was going to knock me down."

"He's a local," the farmer's wife responds. "He won't hurt you."

Her friend makes light of the episode. "Wait till I get back home and tell everyone I was ravaged by a kangaroo."

All too soon it is time to depart. The three say their goodbyes at the back of the town hall. "It was lovely seeing you," she says. And she means it. The visit is something to think about for days. Something to re-live. During his long silences, she will mull over their conversation. And read her treasured novel.

She climbs back into her car, turns the wheel, waves for the last time and steers south. Back she drives to her farm, to her man, to her future.

The Secret

The ceiling is off-white, a crack shaped like a question mark above where she lies; there is a bruise of mould near the naked light bulb. It is stuffy in the room that holds nothing but the double bed and two wooden chairs with chipped paint, one on guard at either side. She continues to look up, tracing the outline of the crack, trying not to think about what is happening. She is transporting herself to another place, away from the sweaty smell of bodies and dusty mattress to the seaside, running across the sand, free as a gull. She can go anywhere – and often does. She has been to America and walked the streets of New York, has been feted by pop stars, appeared in tabloids - on a front page no less - has eaten at the ritziest restaurants and spent an entire evening laying in a bubble bath listening to soothing music. But the trip to the ocean was the best, spending happy hours bobbing about in the water, lying on the sand afterwards with not a worry, feeling the sun brown her body. There was no-one to whom she was responsible; there was only the company of kind people, nights sleeping undisturbed and waking to days that were welcomed and that she wished would never end, though eventually of course they did.

"Go wash yourself," he says later, and she does. She always does what he says. If she doesn't there are consequences, a smack with his open palm across her face, a punch in the stomach, a kick in the head when he has felled her. So now she crouches over the chipped enamel bowl on the bathroom floor and splashes water on to her private parts. He is standing in the doorway watching her, looking down at her budding breasts, the nipples small and puckered, her flat stomach, her pubis with its fine hair.

He has put on a pair of shorts and she can see the livid scar on his chest, a war injury, he once said. Perhaps someone fired a bullet and tried to kill him. Often she lies awake on her narrow bed in the room next to his and imagines herself tiptoeing in the darkness along the hallway, taking the rifle which is perched against the refrigerator there, and sneaking into his room where is sleeping and aiming at his head. She imagines herself squeezing the trigger and watching his body jerk, watching the life draining from him as his blood seeps on to the bedding.

"Hurry up," he snaps, turning away.

When he is gone, she dries herself and dresses in shorts and T-shirt. Then she pads into the kitchen where he is standing at the sink looking through the window at the paddocks beyond.

"Put the kettle on," he says.

It is then that someone knocks on the front door. They are not expecting visitors. In fact, they rarely have visitors and then only on weekends, never during a weekday like today.

He turns and nods at her to see who it is. She is frightened, thinking perhaps it is the police. She wills it to be her parents come to get her. She often dreams of her true mother and father and of them coming to release her from these people whom she knows have abducted her when she was a baby. Her heart thumps wildly.

She pats down her uncombed hair and adjusts her face to greet the caller.

"Jan!" She is shocked to see the woman from the holiday home whom she knows lives a long way away and who she never thought would visit. And, too, she is fearful. Can Jan read her mind, know what she is doing here; know what transpired earlier?

Jan smiles. The girl does not know what to do, whether or not to invite her in. She senses him standing behind her and turns.

He is looking at Jan, his face blank. There is a long pause while the two adults survey one another.

"I'm Jan Christie," the woman says, offering him a business card. He does not take it. "From Howard House."

He knows who she is.

"I called into the school to check on Nancy. And when I found that she was absent, I thought I'd come by to see if she's okay."

Jan sounds so professional, so full of confidence and charm that the girl relaxes.

Another pause. The woman is waiting for an invitation into the house but none is forthcoming.

"Would it be all right if I speak with Nancy?"

He nods acquiescence but his glance at the girl is a warning. Maintain the secret, it says. Shut the fuck up.

The girl is so happy to be allowed out. She follows Jan, admiring her sensible shiny shoes, her matching skirt and jacket, the leather handbag slung over her shoulder. She wants to hold Jan's hand, to let her know how delighted she is that she has travelled so far - 100 kilometres perhaps – to visit her. But she is also filled with trepidation that Jan will ask questions, difficult questions that she will not know how to answer.

They sit in the car parked at the side of the road under eucalypts which are shedding long strips of bark. The car smell is familiar – leather, and Jan's scent. Lavender, perhaps.

"So now you know where I live," the girl says.

They look across the road at the forlorn fibro house, no more than a shack, in a weed-filled yard.

"You weren't at school," the woman says.

The girl can't think of what to say so says nothing.

"What were you doing when I arrived?"

This is easy.

"Putting on the kettle."

"You're not sick?"

"No."

The social worker is looking askance. The girl wishes she could read her mind. She cannot look at her face for fear the truth is written in bold, capital letters in her eyes, or across her forehead, nor fear that the truth will leap from her mouth. She wants to tell, but fear is a powerful deterrent. Besides, even though she feels something akin to love for this woman, she has no experience of trust, and so her lips remain tight. She fiddles with a loose thread from her shorts and wonders how to change the direction of the woman's inquisition.

"Why are you at home, if you're not sick?"

This is so much like school – difficult questions and inescapable corners.

"My dad wanted me to stay home."

"Why?"

Oh, if only she could tell! But not knowing the consequences of truth is too huge, too unknown, to contemplate.

"He wanted me to help him."

The thread is getting longer, pulling apart the stitching. She wants to break it off, but knows it will unravel even further if she does.

"Help to fix the car," she adds when the length of silence becomes too long.

This answer is true: before that - before the bed - the girl had helped her father change tyres.

The woman is used to dealing with lies and secrets and subterfuge. She knows her relationship with the girl is tenuous. She remembers their first meeting at the home, when the girl challenged her authority, and having deflected a tense stand-off then with humour, she observed the girl warming to her. Since the girl left the home she has written to her from time to time. She likes her, appreciates her intelligence, her ambition. She senses the girl has no role model, no friends, and today, seeing her circumstances, knows she is struggling against poverty and ignorance and even, perhaps, against hope. She wants to help the girl to realise her potential.

"Would you like some chocolate?" She opens her handbag and rummages within it.

The girl relaxes, and for the first time lifts her head.

"How come you went to my school?" she asks.

"I was out this way," the woman lies. Truth is, she had no reason to visit the girl. Just instinct. And now she feels there is something going on which is wrong. She tries to make light conversation, but she cannot recapture the camaraderie she and the girl shared when the girl was staying at the home.

She talks about another girl at the home. "Betty... remember her?"

The girl nods.

"She's going to court. To testify against her father."

The girl glances away, looks ahead through the windscreen at the lonely road. "Why?" she asks.

"He was interfering with her."

The girl gives no sign of having heard.

"Do you know what that means?"

"Yes. Of course."

"Do you think she should?"

"What?"

"Testify against her father. For interfering with her."

The girl shrugs. "I don't know," she mumbles.

Once again it is as though an invisible but powerful shield has been dropped between the two of them. There is no way the girl is going to talk. If there is anything to talk about, to reveal.

They chat for a while about school. And then it is time to part.

The girl yearns to go with the woman. The muscles of her heart ache, as though they are straining to breaking point. She feels betrayed, somehow. She wants to plead with the woman, to go with her. Instead, she farewells her politely, standing by the side of the car, talking through the open window.

"Tell your father I said 'goodbye'," the woman says.

"Sure."

And then the car bearing hope is ripping away into the distance until it becomes nothing but empty road.

In the house the father is pottering around the kitchen.

"She gone?" he asks.

"Yes."

"What did she want?"

"She just asked about school."

"Why you weren't there?" He has a mug of tea poised in front of his cruel lips.

She nods.

"And what did you say?"

"That I was helping you mend the car."

The girl feels as though she will burst. She wants to be alone, to cry, to berate herself for not telling the truth, for letting her only hope drive away.

"She's a fucking lesbian," her father says.

"No, she's not!"

The words are out of the girl's mouth before she knows it. A dreadful, cold fear clenches her insides. He is never to be challenged. Never.

But instead of reacting harshly, he's smiling. Sneering. "She's a fucking lesbian, if ever I saw one."

She cannot help herself, she must defend Jan. Her friend. The only person who cares about her.

"No!" She cries the word aloud, angrily. And he does what she knew he would. He swings and smacks her across the face.

She sees stars.

"Fucking lesbian!"

"She's not!" She cannot stop denying it, she needs to defend Jan. She needs to. But he is repeating it again and again. "Fucking lesbian!" And she's yelling at him. And he's whacking her. She's on the floor, sobbing, hurting, saying "no, no, no, no she's not," over and over again. And now he's kicking her. Kicking her stomach, her head. And she squirms and wriggles. Away from him. Away from his ramming foot. And now she's running. Running down the hall, around the corner, wrenching open the back door, flying across the landing, onto the ground, across the yard. Running. And screaming. And sobbing. And he's shouting, calling at her to come back. But she's not coming back. She's going and she's never coming back.

Across the paddock she flees. Her feet don't touch the ground. She doesn't feel the dirt underfoot, the rocks, the twigs, the thorns. All she knows is fear. She has answered him back, questioned his authority. She has welcomed death for he will kill her if he catches her. She is nothing but fear and movement, she is running fast, fast, fast!

Something whizzes past her. A bullet! She half-turns as she runs and sees him, lumbering after her with the rifle. He's going to shoot her, fell her, end her life. She keeps running, faster, faster, faster!

Under the fence she throws herself. Does not feel the wire rip into the flesh. Only feels the bullet ripping her open. Up and on, into the bush, past trees and shrubs, running, leaping, moving, getting away, fast, fast, fast!

How much later it is that she stops she cannot tell. She is out of breath, bending over and panting, the blood pounding in her head, her chest hot and wheezy. At last she has outrun him.

She falls upon the ground, curls into a foetal shape and sobs. She wants her mother. Her true mother. The mother she seeks all of her days, the mother who will hold her close, promise her protection eternally. She sees her mother now, dreams her into existence as she has done at other times when the man has terrified her. This is a mother who is stronger than him. Stronger than any man, stronger than the world!

Time passes. The crying time has passed. She is alone now, deep in the bush and wondering what she should now do. She cannot go back, for he will, without doubt, murder her. As much as she hates her life, she does not want to be murdered. What she wants is Jan. Why didn't she tell Jan when she had the chance? She could have driven off in the car with Jan. Could have escaped the man who says he is her father, who is no father, who is the most terrible of all terrors.

Her mind calms. Her breathing is now controlled, and she is no longer anxious. In fact, a calmness has come over her. There is only one solution: she will find Jan and tell her and trust her to know what to do.

She stands and, her feet bleeding, she limps through the bush, heading in the direction in which she thinks the main road to town leads. She doesn't know how to get to where Jan lives, nor does she know how to get to the holiday home where Jan works. But now she has devised her plan, she is confident that the way will become clear.

It takes some time, but eventually she leaves the bush and walks across paddocks and finds the road. There is not much traffic at this time of the day, but surely someone will pick her up and drive her into town. From there she will catch a train to the city. And from there...? She's still not sure. But she can do it, she must.

A car is approaching. She hooks her thumb for a ride, but the driver ignores her and speeds past. She plods along, still limping, exhausted. Another car passes her. And another. For a long while no-one else travels the road.

Then she turns at the sound of an approaching engine. It is her worst nightmare: it is him and he's speeding towards her. She wants to run again but all of a sudden her energy deserts her. She is tired, so tired, tireder than she has ever been in her life. And trapped, too, trapped by years of being his victim.

He pulls up alongside of her. The window is down.

"Get in," he says.

She shakes her head, limps on.

He cruises alongside her. She glances into the car. She cannot see the gun.

"Get in," he repeats, braking.

His voice is a magnet that says he must be obeyed. She opens the door and slides into the seat.

Her head is throbbing. She cannot look at him.

There is something she must say, something she has never said before, though she cannot think why not.

"If you ever touch me again, I will tell the police." Her voice is soft but loud enough for him to know she is speaking the truth.

He does not answer, makes no signal that he has even heard. He turns the steering wheel and drives back in the direction from which he has come.

Other People's Children

Ramona has the sock poised over her chubby foot when the child sees what she's doing. 'Not now!' Chelsea screams. 'No! No!'

Not for the first time Ramona wonders if her three-year-old granddaughter has Asperger's, like her father. She met Chelsea three days earlier, having travelled from Australia to Montreal where her daughter, Mandy, now lives, happily married – or so it seems – to French-Canadian, Jean-Pierre. Ramona was thrilled to be a granny for the first time and excited about finally meeting Chelsea. But the child is a disappointment.

'No!' Chelsea snaps when Ramona goes to kiss her.

'No' to hugs and handholding.

When Ramona tries to help dress Chelsea, the child tells her, in no uncertain terms, 'When I'm ready!'

Used to other people's children responding positively to her, Ramona is puzzled. Among her friends with children or grandchildren, she is known as 'the kid whisperer', and generations of youngsters she's taught have adored her. But her only child Mandy has always been difficult, and now it seems history is repeating itself with this willful granddaughter.

It is a strained visit. Mandy and Jean-Pierre did not meet her at the airport, did not offer to drive her to their city-outskirts duplex. Even when Ramona arrives at their home, jet-lagged but full of good cheer, their greetings are lukewarm, less than she had expected.

Ramona remembers her last visit, before the birth of her grandchild.

It was the first day after she'd arrived. Exhausted from long air travel hours, she had slept in. When she awoke, the house was still and empty. A note lay on the kitchen table along with house keys. 'Jean-Pierre's at work. I've gone for a job interview. Mandy.'

Ramona made herself a cup of tea, poked about in cupboards for something to eat – it was obvious the family did not eat breakfast cereal – made a slice of toast, and then dressed.

Goodness knows when Mandy will be home, she thought. I might as well go for a walk, look at the neighbourhood. She checked that all the doors were locked and was exiting when the house alarm started, an ear-piercing sound. Ramona rushed to the panel on the kitchen wall and stood there, trying to work out what to do. She poked a few buttons, but the alarm continued shrieking. Next, she looked around for an instruction manual or the alarm company's phone number. There were stacks of children's books, scraps of paper, clothing and more, but not a phone or an address book.

The alarm continued, loud and insistent. Ramona rushed around, not sure what to do next. Used to being in control, she was more than anxious – was even panicking. The neighbours — perhaps they could help! Ramona rushed to the next-door house, thumping on the front door. Nobody answered. She got the same lack of response from the houses on the other side of Mandy's place. And the two houses across the road, nobody was home. And wouldn't you want to know it; the street was deserted of people whom she could ask for help.

Exasperated, Ramona stomped back to her daughter's house. The alarm was still shrilling. By now, tears began to fall. Why hadn't she noticed the panel and realised the house was alarmed? Why hadn't Mandy left instructions in case of an emergency like this? She sat on the steps leading from the kitchen to the side of the house, put her head in her hands and sobbed. What else was there to do? It was a long time since she had felt so helpless, so hopeless.

She was still sobbing when Jean-Pierre arrived. His bicycle braked near Ramona's foot. She looked up, silently thanking God for the unexpected saviour.

'I'm so sorry, Jean-Pierre,' she said, 'I didn't know the alarm was on. And I didn't know how to unalarm it.' She knew that the word 'unalarm' wasn't the right word, but she was too upset to think of what it ought to be.

Jean-Pierre seemed not to notice her there or to hear her. He went straight to the alarm panel and punched buttons. The shrilling stopped and a peace reigned in the house. At last.

'I'm so sorry,' Ramona repeated. 'Sorry you had to leave work to attend to this.'

'It's okay,' Jean-Pierre mumbled.

'Let me pay for a taxi for you to go back to work,' Ramona offered.

'It's okay,' her son-in-law repeated. Then, without another word, he went outside, mounted his bike and rode off.

Like Mandy when she was a child, Chelsea is an attractive girl with straight flaxen hair, cut in a bob, and a fringe that frames her pixie-shaped face. Mandy's eyes are green, but Chelsea's are like her father's – dark brown and intense. Ramona sees the future adult in her granddaughter's face, self-assured and intelligent, used to being in charge. Mandy never had that assurance: as a small child, she was always anxious, fearful of new experiences, of strangers, of unfamiliar places. And, too, Mandy's behaviour was passive, although there is no evidence of that nowadays.

'You dry and Jean-Pierre will wash,' she says, thrusting a towel at Ramona after the first meal. 'I've calls to make.'

Ramona watches her daughter stride into her office, Chelsea trailing her.

In the time that follows, Jean-Pierre applies himself almost religiously to the task, treating each dirty vessel or implement as something sacred, to be scrupulously washed, then rinsed, then laid neatly in its place on the rack. He doesn't acknowledge Ramona as she wipes the dinner dishes, laying them on the kitchen table, rather than – as she would at a friend's place – asking where they ought to go — she is afraid Jean-Pierre might ignore her question. She feels as though she ought to try at conversation, but her son-in-law is so engrossed in his cleaning, she remains silent, not even daring to hum to herself, which she does at home while drying up.

After he empties the sink and wipes down the benches, Jean-Pierre takes the dried crockery and stacks it in cupboards, puts cutlery in drawers and pots in their places. Studiously avoiding Ramona's gaze, he wipes his hands and leaves the room.

Ramona wonders if Jean-Pierre is plain rude or if Mandy has spoken disparagingly about her and he's being loyal. She wishes she was back home in Australia. It was silly to make this trip, to try to find some peace with her daughter. The rift between them – begun when Ramona was a single mother and Mandy a rebellious teenager — is now a valley that can never be filled. Yes, it is too late. Mandy belongs to this strange, solemn man. And he deserves her. These are the thoughts Ramona takes to the lounge-room where there is no television, only Jean-Pierre and Mandy quietly reading. She asks a few questions about Mandy's work, her health, anything that Mandy might respond to happily, but Mandy is more interested in her book.

'Well, I'll be off to bed, then,' Ramona says.

'Oh, okay Mum,' says Mandy, looking up. 'See you in the morning.'

The bed in the spare room is comfortable but the room is sparse and impersonal. Ramona pulls up the doona, and lies there in the dark, thinking about the day. She misses home where there is none of this tiptoeing around, where she can speak her mind.

It is Saturday, and Mandy and Jean-Pierre are taking Chelsea to the Museum.

'She knows most of the planets now, in the correct order from the sun,' Mandy boasts. 'Chelsea, tell Aussie Nana the planets.'

Sitting at the kitchen table, Chelsea continues drawing with crayon on a sheet of paper. She appears to have not heard.

Mandy smiles. 'Too busy. Maybe later.'

The four of them trudge along the windswept street to the bus stop. Ramona notices that today Chelsea has both her parents' hands as they walk, a promising sign.

Climbing aboard, Chelsea insists on inserting everyone's passes into the bus's ticket machine; this holds up the queue of passengers. The bus driver looks annoyed and glances at his watch. But Mandy and Jean-Pierre are patient, and then proud when Chelsea succeeds.

In the bus, Ramona enjoys looking at the passing scenery. It is autumn and the trees are dropping leaves. Autumn back home isn't as obvious as here in Canada, she thinks. Chelsea is sitting opposite her between her parents, staring at her. Ramona grins at her granddaughter, but she does not respond. Regardless, she continues making eye contact with Chelsea and smiling until the little girl twists around and kneels to look out of the window with her back to her. Mandy and Jean-Pierre are talking to one another over Chelsea's head. Ramona wonders what they might be talking about. Their conversation to one another in her presence has been mostly directional – 'will you please put out the bins', 'can I have the book you were reading' and so on.

They have arrived at their destination, Montreal's main street. As they alight, Chelsea swinging by the arms, held by her father, Ramona sees a large sign which looks as though it is important. Her French is poor – in fact Chelsea had said to her mother the night before, 'Aussie Nana speaks funny French,' – so she catches up with Mandy and says, 'What does it say on that sign back there?'

Mandy swings around, glares at Ramona, and snaps, 'God, you overwhelm me sometimes, you really do!'

Ramona is flummoxed. And deeply wounded. All morning she has done exactly what Mandy wanted, and more – put clothes in the washing machine, tidied the kitchen, picked up mess from the floor and washed breakfast dishes. She has scarcely talked. This attack of Mandy's is not unprecedented, but usually it's in a context; this time it's come out of nowhere. Mandy walks ahead. Ramona does not follow; instead, she finds a nearby bench and sits down, stares at passersby, wishes to hell she was back at home.

She sits there until Chelsea wanders up. 'Aussie Nana,' the child says, 'Mummy wants you.'

Ramona looks at the child. She is so pretty, so smartly dressed, and she seems like a normal little girl. She doesn't say anything, just stares at Chelsea who stares back at her.

At least she's making eye contact, thinks Ramona. God, she's so like her mother. Unlikeable. Selfish. Self-centred.

Goodness, what am I thinking? Ramona gulps. Fancy thinking these things of a little girl, only three years old. She remonstrates with herself and smiles at Chelsea who frowns, then turns and scampers away.

Later Mandy loops her arms around her mother's shoulder. 'I'm sorry, Mum,' she says.

'Sometimes you overwhelm me, too,' Ramona replies. She wants to say that it was practically the first time all day she'd spoken to Mandy; that she is trying so hard to be pleasant and accommodating. But for now, it's enough that Mandy realises she had been unreasonable.

'Anyway, where are we going now?' Ramona asks.

It is a week later, a difficult week during which Ramona is on her best behaviour, trying not to be in any way intrusive. She has taken Mandy shopping and bought her daughter Manchester for the new bed she and Jean-Pierre have just bought – sheets, pillows and cases, doona and cover. Jean-Pierre complains how hard the new pillows are, but

Ramona is delighted to be sleeping 'with lovely fresh bedding' and no longer on a mattress on the floor.

On the last night Ramona packs her bags and bids her farewells. 'I've ordered the taxi for 2 am,' she says. 'I'll leave quietly, so best to say goodbye here.'

For the first time, her granddaughter kisses her. On the cheeks and at her mother's bidding, but it is still a kiss and she says goodbye. In French – 'au revoir'. Avoiding eye contact, Jean-Pierre shakes Ramona's hand and Mandy gives her a gracious hug and says cheerfully, 'I hope you have a good trip back to Australia.'

Outdoors, early next morning, notwithstanding the streetlights, it is dark. Quiet and still. Ramona sits with her bags on the front step leading up to Mandy's verandah, her feet planted on the footpath. The taxi is a few minutes late but there is plenty of time before the plane leaves.

'I'm going to kill you! Kill you all!' A man's voice is calling from not very far away. It seems to be coming towards Ramona, a crazed voice repeating the threat again and again.

Fearful that she is the intended target of the death threat, Ramona shuffles back into the dark of the verandah, edging as close as she can to Mandy's front door. Her bags sit on the footpath but there is no way on earth she's going to lean forward to collect them and be seen.

'Yes, I'll kill you!'

The voice is closer. And there, suddenly, is its owner, a tall young man with dark, disheveled hair. The streetlight illuminates his features. He pauses, glances to his right and sees Ramona looking up at him.

'Hello,' says Ramona, her voice cracking.

'Hello,' he replies, as friendly as an old mate or a next door neighbour. He continues walking and calling, 'I'll kill you! Kill you!' as he passes further along the street.

A minute later, when the threats can no longer be heard, the taxi arrives.

'Where are you headed to?' the driver asks.

'Home,' says Ramona. 'Australia.' There is nowhere else she'd rather be.

My Boy Luke

The first time you meet Luke he's at Moya's, his current foster carer. He's the tallest one who Moya's three screaming boys climb over, who sits and grins at you as if to say, "I was made for being trodden on."

You take Luke to your home and watch as he wanders around, checking out your paintings, your books, your tidily packed pantry. You listen as he says, "Cool." This is his biggest compliment. He tells you how much he likes your home because it is quiet and peaceful. He wants peace, so much, this little nine-year-old boy with the shy smile and mop of curly brown hair.

At the end of his first visit, you give Luke your phone number, but he doesn't ring. Moya wouldn't let him phone he says next time he comes for respite care. He also says that Moya has taken her three to the circus that week and he had to stay home with her partner who smokes and drinks and yells all the time. Luke tells you this as a matter of fact, without sounding accusatory or sorry for himself: it's just the way his life is.

You find out more about Luke from his case worker, how he was homeless for 12 months with his mother. Now you understand why, when he gets into your car, he immediately clicks shut all the door locks. He's used to sleeping in cars, and in rooms where his mother is selling her body. You learn that he was finally taken from her because at a drug party she'd OD'd and he, aged six, was the only one sensible enough to ring triple O.

As the weeks pass and you bring Luke home on weekends, "to give Moya a break", you teach him how to eat at a table, how to set that table, how to sit still and to read, how to shop for groceries. You watch his delight the first time you're in a supermarket and you tell him he can choose whichever foods he most likes. He thinks you're lying: he's used to people lying to him.

At night you tuck him into the new bed you bought, just for him, with its quilt you spent hours helping him choosing, and, as he falls to sleep after you've read to him, you stroke his hair and kiss his toast-warm cheek. He smiles as he falls asleep, though sometimes he awakes, sweaty and frightened, from a nightmare.

Within weeks, Luke is telling Moya he doesn't want to live with her anymore. And Moya's telling him she doesn't want him. The welfare people ring and tell you that Luke is - for the tenth time – being offered for fostering. He wants no other foster parents but you. There's five days to make a decision.

It's five days of ceaseless discussion between you and your husband who have spent ten years thinking of getting a dog, and still don't have one. You weigh the pros and cons. You've long passed the age of fifty; you're used to sustained periods alone with no family obligations; you have a perfectly happy relationship with one another. But then...

Before you know it, you're speaking to Luke's mother who's in custody in the police station next door to the courthouse where the hearing's to be held. She barely says a word, doesn't ask about us, whether we care for her boy Luke. In fact, she seems bored. Or perhaps she's coming down from whatever drug feeds her body.

In the courthouse Luke's caseworker whispers that his father is seated across from us. You smile at him, but he ignores you. There's a woman holding his hand. Later you are to learn that she is Luke's stepmother and the reason why Luke doesn't live with his father is that she has said, "It's the boy or me" and his father has chosen her.

Now you're in court and the magistrate is saying he's had a chat with Luke and has found him one of the nicest children he's ever met. Your heart swells with pride and childishly you cross your fingers and hope that you will get this sweet boy for your very own. You remember the irony of your first birth, when all through the hours of pain you believed that the child you were carrying was a boy, and you were going to call him Luke. You gave birth instead to a girl, Claire, who is now a woman and a Canadian citizen, and later to Kathleen, dead at the age of two.

When the magistrate announces that Luke is now your foster son until the age of 18, you bawl with gratitude. He is then — and forever — embroidered on your heart.

Murderous Thoughts

The rifle with its long, dangerous barrel rests against the ever-humming fridge. Every day she notes it there, waiting like an accomplice, biding its time. Sometimes she takes it with her, stalking across paddocks into the bush. There she practices shooting at objects – a dead branch dangling from a tree, tin cans she sets up on a stump. Now and again a rabbit scuttles through the undergrowth and she raises the rifle, squints through the view-finder and gently squeezes the trigger. The bullets never find their mark. It is as though the weapon has not yet found its true target.

Lately an idea has been scratching at her brain. It is an idea that if acted upon has unimaginable consequences. But still it persists. Sometimes it pokes hard and her stomach grips with the enormity of the thought. What if she followed through on the idea and failed? The thought is terrifying, and she is not brave. As she moves about the kitchen the rifle seems to salute her, seems to shout, "Do it! I'm willing!" and she has to avert her eyes and focus her mind on other matters.

Today he has commandeered her and her sister. He has decided that the back paddock should be ploughed for the planting of potatoes. He has bought a plough, the sort a horse might pull – metal, with wide-apart arms that curve down to a blade. Instead of a horse to harness the plough they have a car, old and with running boards, unregistered, that they drive across the paddocks.

'Get that cable and hook it onto the fender, Nancy,' he commands.

She runs to obey. He ties two ropes to each side of the plough and the other end of the ropes to a loop at the plough-end of the cable.

'Valda, get in the car and start it up,' he says. 'Nancy, you stand

here..." He gestures for her to position herself behind the plough. '...
and hold the handles.'

His daughters obey.

'Now, Valda, put it into first gear, and gently touch the accelerator.'

The car revs, smoke blows out of its muffler. Then it is moving forward. Holding onto the plough handles, Nancy is jerked forward so fast her feet barely touch the earth. Within moments the plough encounters a buried stump and flies high up into the air. Nancy trips, falls forward, her chin contacting the bar where the ropes are tied, and she lands face-first into a furrow the plough has made.

The car continues moving ahead, her sister oblivious to the accident. She hears her father screaming abuse, screaming at Valda to stop the car, screaming at her to get up.

Her jaw aches, she has seen stars as she landed, but she obeys instantly.

'You fucking idiot!' He is standing over her, his eyes bulbous, his jaw working like a machine, his hands fisted. She struggles to arise, and as she does so, he swings at her. His fist smashes against her face and once again she sees stars.

'Didn't you see the fucking stump?'

She's not sure if he is questioning her or her sister. But it seems he doesn't expect an answer for now he is demanding that they both take their places and resume the ploughing. 'And fucking do it right this time!' he screams.

This time Valda drives the car more slowly, easing it at the end of the paddock to allow her to turn, and to continue eastwards. At the back of the car the plough churns up the soil and behind it Nancy runs, panting and hot-faced. Out of the corner of her eye she notices that their father is standing up a tree, lifting a bottle of water to his mouth.

Her head is throbbing, and her jaw. She would like to explore it with her fingers, feel if the bone is broken. But her hands are needed to guide the plough.

It is only when the paddock is ploughed that she and her sister take a break. He doesn't comment on the job that they have done, just gets them to unhook the plough and tie on the scarifier, a metal grid with spikes that will break up the earthen clods. He allows them to drink some water and then they continue the job.

How much longer, an hour or two, and they have finished to his satisfaction. He sends them to the house for lunch.

'What have you been doing?' asks their mother. 'It's three o'clock.' She gives them sandwiches and notices that her daughter's face is bruised. 'Are you okay?' she asks.

Nancy nods. 'Yes.' She's never sure that her mother truly cares if she's hurt. She walks from the kitchen to the dining table and notices the rifle. It is standing there, offering an invitation that is now irresistible. As she sits and chews the meal, her jaw painful and tears pricking the backs of her eyes, the thought becomes so big she knows it is just a matter of time.

Mother, Mother

The week Brian's mother died, my daughter Karen left home. It was the same week I found a lump in my breast. She'd been planning to go for a long time, meeting friends in secret, conspiring whenever I was absent. She visited the local housing co-operative and the Department of Social Security. At sixteen, she was obviously capable.

She went suddenly. No-one suspected her bad heart. She was always on the go, rarely complained of tiredness. When the attack came, Catherine called for Brian. He worked on the porch where she had fallen, massaging her tired chest. And she recovered, for a while at least, hooked to machines in the hospital. When she died, Brian said, she had a look of utter peace on her face. She was seventy years old.

The lump was small, gristly. I felt it under the shower one morning; didn't think much about it at the time. Karen was on my mind so much that week. She was away at a school camp for a few days. I kept telling myself that before long she would stop locking herself away, sulking and raging at my existence, despising everything I represented.

It was peaceful with her gone. I studied for my university exams – Woolfe, Conrad, Mansfield. I liked Mansfield's work best. Her writing was simple but with subtext; you had to search for clues. The conflict in her stories was understated but ever-present. I identified with her characters and their dilemmas, how they tried to find expression for deep feelings. Read 'The Daughters of the Later Colonel' over and over. When her mother died, I thought Catherine would react like the Colonel's daughters to their father's death – grieving and exploring future possibilities but bound by habit to routine, to the familiar, to home and family. Catherine was still living with the old lady up until her death. Who or what would she turn to? Unmarried and over forty, had never dated.

Karen returned when I was out attending lectures. I'd left her a note, explaining I'd be home soon, also that there was chocolate cake in the pantry. A goodwill gesture, I'd made the cake that morning. My mind was less jumbled now. Time had ironed out troubles, had neatly folded new compromises. We would have another talk and resolve our differences now that we'd had a week apart from each other. We could start again and be happy in our lives together. The lump, though, was still in my breast. Was it my imagination, or had it grown?

Karen wasn't home when I returned from Uni. She'd eaten the cake. I CAN'T WAIT, she'd written as a postscript to my note. VANESSA AND I ARE LOOKING FOR A FLAT.

So, it has come to this, I thought, dark and bruised. For endless days I have courted you with anxious duty – this in the name of Mother. The very word weighs heavily upon me. I evoke the picture of my own mother, rigid with resentment and rejection at her monster-child, thief of her future. But for her weak, willing flesh, the vice of motherhood – but for me – she could have been a star, her name in flashing neon lights all over the world. My mother, the would-be dancer, was always the mother.

Once I had tried to work miracles for her. She rejected grand gestures, so I gave, with hope, small but frequent tokens of affection: gave my time to her demands without murmur, even when it was inconvenient, even though I had my own husband and child to care for. It was an unrewarded, this duty of daughter. She always took and rarely acknowledged my giving. And so a fire entered into me, and in the end it burned itself out and nothing remained in my heart for her. No longer caring, I abandoned her to the mother shell of illusion she clung to. Later, much later, like the narrator in the *Heart of Darkness*, she would cry, 'The horror!' The horror!' but it was too late to turn back — too late. The journey was ended; I could embark on the next.

And now, for a fleeting moment, like that before eminent death, I saw all so clearly what it was all about. The clouds slid apart. I saw a common roof binding my daughter and I, but little else. Between generations of my family's blood, past and present, there is no premise of love, nothing taken for granted. Love has to be earned in this frail, fragmentary family. We have no tradition to lean upon: we need to invent and construct our own prototypes.

But there was I, an amateur, with no gift for miracles. I felt exhausted, beyond all caring. In encroaching darkness, I sat in my living room reflecting upon whether or not it was a myth that we become forever responsible for what we have created. More than ever, like Woolfe, I needed a room of my own.

I touched the lump. It was bigger, begging to be cut out. Exorcised (or was it excised? The right word failed me.)

She went, with her friends all around her. The local church was packed with housewives, bowlers from her club, a bishop, shop-keepers, neighbours, children, grand-children. The ceremony was Catholic and long — the ritual of departure from this world. Catherine wept and held Brian's hand throughout. So did Shirley, the other daughter. I felt awkward, not belonging to this intimacy. When the Communion was celebrated, the daughters went forward eagerly. I thought Brian would go too though he was not religious like the rest of his family. It would have been a grand gesture at such a crucial time. But he stayed where he was in the pew, tears streaming down his face.

The pulse of hymns that she had loved so well grew faint, and died.

Nobody at the wake asked where Karen was. She had refused to go. When the phone rang to announce the old lady's death, she'd taken the call and then presented me with the news, seeming to be bemused as though she didn't care. And she probably didn't. What was someone's else's mother to her? What was her own?

Brian loved his mother. And she idolized him. Every day he drove home from work to have lunch with her. She owned a greyhound, a thin, aging bitch racked with nervous complaints, barely able to walk. Whenever she went to bowls, the old lady would leave the back door open so it could go in and out of the house. And she'd leave on the radio, tuned to the greyhound races. Brian, Catherine, Shirley and the dog, they were her life. She dug earth, planted seed, shaped clay into useful pots, celebrated new growth and laughed. She was the mother of all mothers.

In the dark I sat for hours, waiting for Karen. I thought she might at least have consulted me before searching for new diggings. The past – and present – breathed heavily upon my face. What did she care that old lady was dead. That Brian was grieving, that my breast had a lump, that exams were looking and that, trying to find reasons for the way she treated me, I couldn't sleep. And where had I left that love which was once so generous for her? I had loved her passionately when she was small and needy. Lately I had wanted to return that affection, but now it was buried too deep in my heart of darkness, smothered by family traditions, her self-centeredness and my own cynicism.

When she returned, slamming doors, presenting the back of her head, ignoring me, I did the only thing I was capable of by then. My hand struck her defiant face, left a red mark on her cheek. Her eyes registered astonishment. A heavy foot – was it mine? – thudded into the small of her back. I saw her look of terror. Somehow a shoe came adrift. I found it in my hand and whacked the side of her head with it. I was beyond words.

So, this is motherhood, I wanted to say but was incapable. This is where it goes when it has ended.

She is screaming, racing for the door, limping. I hear her wailing all the way down the street, the wail of the grief-stricken who knows there is no turning back.

She is dead now. The mother buried. It is no use trying to resurrect her for she will never be forgiven. The wounds of past form scars. The relatives have departed. Have fled. Which rhymes with dread, with dead, with all's said.

The Survivor

She told me her name was Sylvie and she was five years old and then she showed me her collection of decapitated china dolls. Looking like one of her them with her pale, porcelain complexion, attractive blue eyes framed by long lashes, and rosebud lips, she did not seem at all perturbed that her mother, Jessica, had moments before been marched to the police car in handcuffs. Nor was she concerned that paramedics had taken the body of her sister Jasmine to the morgue. She seemed even less interested in the blood that covered her from her long blonde hair to the front of her pyjamas and over her face and hands. The dolls were what most interested her. She picked up one of the doll's heads and kissed it, leaving a bloodied mark from her lips on its cheek and then looked steadfastly at me.

'Who took off the heads?' I asked gently.

She smiled at me with a look that was both beguiling and challenging at the same time.

'Was it you?' I prodded.

She paused, seeming to decide if I was worth speaking to. Then she gave an almost imperceptible nod, her smile widening, like a challenge.

As a police forensic psychologist, I had been tasked with interviewing the mother's surviving daughter about her sister Jasmine's death to find what Sylvie knew. She seemed to have no outward reaction to the murder of her sister, whose throat and abdomen had been slashed. I wondered how she had gotten so much blood on herself. Her home, too, was teeming with police, but she seemed oblivious.

There was a silence the length of a heartbeat and then, in a voice as meek as a mouse, she said, 'Will I live with you now?' Her eyes fixed on my face as she gave what I guessed was her best begging puppy dog look.

'Someone will come for you soon,' I said. 'She will take you to a foster mother who will look after you. I'm sure you will really like her.'

Her face had the expression then of someone who had inhaled a nasty smell. I wondered what on earth was going through her tiny brain.

'Do you want to tell me more about your dollies?' I asked.

'No,' she replied, her tone of voice indicating that discussion on the topic was closed. I got the impression that, once she realised I wasn't taking her to my home, she had dismissed me.

As delicately as I could, I asked her a few questions about what had happened earlier in the house. Had she seen her mother with a knife? Where was she when Jasmine was attacked? But now she clamped her lips together and avoided eye contact.

Eventually she spoke. 'I don't know,' she replied when I asked her about the blood on her clothes and body.

Shortly after, a welfare officer arrived, and Sylvie, her eyes suddenly wrinkling up with a smile, took her hand and, without a backward glance at me, toddled off to the waiting car.

Over the weeks that followed, thoughts of Sylvie scratched away at the edges of my thoughts. I absorbed as much as I could about the murder from the media. It seemed that Sylvie's mother was well-regarded and that neighbours were shocked to learn she was charged with the murder of her younger daughter. Jasmine, I read, was two years old and developmentally delayed but the mother always kept her – and Sylvie – immaculately dressed and well-cared for. She had been arraigned for murder in the first degree.

I spoke to my colleague Don Jenkins, a detective on the case. 'Jessica's fingerprints were on the knife,' he said. 'And she's confessed.'

'What about Sylvie?' I asked. 'Where was she when the mother killed the child?'

'According to Jessica, she was in bed asleep, and didn't see anything,' Jenkins replied.

'Strange that she was covered with blood.'

'The mother claimed Sylvie cradled Jasmine after the death. She said she even kissed her sister. Hence the blood on her lips and face.'

I remembered the kiss Sylvie had laid on the face of her doll's decapitated head. Perhaps she had been re-enacting what the mother had said of her kissing her dead sister's face.

'Do you suppose I could interview the foster parents?' I asked.

Jenkins thought it a good idea and told me he would ask his superior. 'I'm sure you will be called to give evidence when the trial comes to court,' he said.

Within a week I was sitting in a comfy chair talking with Kim Ferrier, Sylvie's foster mother. Sylvie, she said, was on a visit to her mother in prison. She had been twice previously.

'What is she like when she comes back from the visit?' I asked.

Mrs Ferrier looked around the room as if seeking an answer. 'She's an odd little girl,' she said at last. 'Not at all demonstrative. When I ask her about her mother, she clams up. The officer who takes her to the prison says that Sylvie's mother dotes on her. But Sylvie doesn't seem at all interested in her mother. She rarely speaks. Not even to ask when her mother will be coming home.'

'You would expect a five-year-old to want her mother,' I mused.

'She seems detached from everyone and everything,' Mrs Ferrier said. 'But there's been trouble at school...'

'Yes?'

'Reports of her bullying other children. And I suspect…'

Mrs Ferrier hesitated. She seemed to want to say something but was debating whether to continue.

'I need to write a report,' I said. 'Everything you can tell me is helpful.'

After a thoughtful moment, the foster mother said, 'It's the cat.'

I nodded.

'Usually Timmy's very playful. But twice I've heard it yowl and run from Sylvie. I haven't seen anything. But I've wondered if she's harming it. The fact is that Timmy won't have anything to do with her. And that's so unusual.'

My visit concluded, I went to my office to write my report. And then I was assigned a new case, one which involved a man with Asperger's who had killed his long-suffering mother. I heard no more about Sylvie until a month later. She was assigned a new foster parent who called me one day.

'The child killed our cat,' she said. 'And the next night I awoke in my bed to find her standing alongside me with a knife raised. I was lucky in being able to tussle it from her hand.'

Years Later

Sunday afternoon I peel potatoes for dinner; finger the hard, dirty tubers under chilled tap water, and think of you.

Sunday back then was always the last day of grieving, the day before we met each week. I could scarcely wait for Monday, for the sight of your face, for the holiness of your arms around me.

Sundays always found me imagining you in in your home. Laughing. Relaxing. Playing with your daughter. Perhaps you peeled potatoes as I did.

A stranger at a self-help meeting led me to you. My need was dire, I said. The woman – whose name I've long forgotten – praised you effusively, made you sound like goddess and miracle worker in one Almighty package. I needed a miracle.

'Helen will help you,' the stranger said.

That first meeting I liked you on sight. Your hair, light brown with traces of grey and whipped into a bun, wisps of hair escaping, as though you had no time for grooming, only time for those in need. Your eyes captivated me, so blue, like looking into the future; and lively. In that sterile waiting room with its white tiles, the clock clicking loudly when we met, you laughed. I knew then you were the one.

Here is the room, square and small, like millions of rooms all over the world. When we sit together this room becomes my universe. You are the Sun and I am a tiny speck in the vastness of space, a speck that grows bigger in your company.

It seems you are always smiling. You warm every minute part of my being with your mouth.

At first you talk a lot. About your life. Like me, you are a swimmer. You love to bodysurf. And to fish. Your father taught you. But now he is dead, and you grieve his passing. You tell me how sometimes you sit in the grotto in the hospital grounds to think about and honour him: it is there, you've told me, that you most feel close.

After our session I too sit in the grotto, which is dark and smells of dampness, trying to relive your closeness. But the grotto air is chilly and uninspiring.

My father was nothing like yours. He is the root of my problems, his abuse, his violence. Weeks later I begin to talk about him, teasing out scraps of information so you can see what it was like back then. Tell how I lived through my childhood years in fear and isolation. And I, too, I tell you about that cold fish, my mother. How she refused the truth, even when I spoke it.

One day I ask if you will hold me. To have your arms around me is all that I want. I become obsessed with the idea. I know that when you hold me, when your arms embrace me, you will hold me together, like the strongest glue.

You say you will think about my request.

I wait.

And wait.

I ask again. And then, to my utter amazement, you agree.

How can I explain the beginning of my life at that time? It is as though God has put all of eternity into place and I am at the very centre of his masterpiece. As I have dreamed, you manage to bring together my fragmented self. Held close to you, I am, for the first moment in my life, complete.

Nothing, of course, is forever perfect. Once you have held me and I have known ecstasy, I desire it again and again. It's like a drug, this wanting to be held, to feel you so close.

And then the downside: you know what you did – the holding — is wrong. You know that I want it forever.

You take a step back. You refuse.

Abandoned, I choke with the pain of your rejection.

I beg.

And again.

You will not relent.

Now I need you more than I could ever have imagined.

Mondays – only one day a week - are not enough. I want you every second of every day. Time without you is endless.

I find out where you live. I go to your home, stand on the road, and look at where you and your daughter live.

But this is not enough. I return, wander around your home, peering through locked windows. Take pieces of you that you've not given. Take them with me to inspect again when I am in my own home, so far away from you.

And of course, I must confess.

How can I not have known that you would be angry? That you would rant at me? Accuse me of betrayal?

I stand in the smallest corner I can find, clamp my fingers to my ears. My heart splinters into thousands of hard, sharp shards.

That night I take a razor and slash my skin. The pain of the flesh compared to the pain of my heart is nothing. Nothing. My mind is splintered, cannot contain rational thought; is more fragmented than ever. You will never hold me. You despise me. You snarled at me. You became a monster, you who are my Mother.

I am mad with pain and rejection.

Hospital.

Alone.

Where are you?

Have you forgiven me?

I spin and spin. Nothing is stable. I cannot begin to understand anything.

This is my life.

Alone.

Abandoned.

There is nothing else.

When will I ever see you again?

Days pass, the seconds click over and over - forever, it seems. Yes, you see me again. But now it is changed. All that is between us is now solid, impenetrable, where once was life-sustaining air.

I write you poems, craft trinkets with every ounce of skill and loving I can muster.

But.

Nothing I can say or do recovers our bond. Never again will I know your arms, your warm words.

I seek the mother you once were to me, but you are as remote as a planet not yet discovered.

It is over.

The truth I told has severed that which was so precious between us; my breaking of trust has turned you into a stranger.

Our parting is absolute.

Weeks pass.

Months.

Years.

Forever.

I ache.

When will the pain recede? Will it ever?

One late Sunday afternoon a decade and more later, I am still thinking of you, remembering your white, smooth arms. The smell of our closeness. The tiny scar on your forehead.

I turn off the tap, discard the peel; slice into virgin potato flesh. White sap bleeds onto the board.

Where is the family-sized pot for cooking and the promise of a meal with enough left over for tomorrow?

THE END